CONTENTS

MAMA AND PAPA BEAR were going out. But cubs Brother and Sister Bear didn't complain. The reason was that their sitter was the one and only Mrs. Grizzle.

Mrs. Grizzle could do all kinds of fun things. She was a whiz at tiddlywinks, she could make a cat's cradle with a bit of string, and she could play the piano and yodel.

But the cubs' favorite thing about Mrs. Grizzle was her bedtime stories.

"Well, what's it going to be tonight?" she asked as she tucked the cubs in. Honey Bear was already asleep in her crib downstairs. Now it was bedtime for Brother and Sister.

"You say," said Sister.

"Okay," said Mrs. Grizzle. "How about 'The Three Little Cubs and the Big Bad Pig'? I'll wager you've never heard of that one before."

"Tell it! Tell it!" cried the cubs.

The Three Little Cubs
and the Big Bad Pig

"Once upon a time," began Mrs. Grizzle, "there were three little cubs who lived with their mother."

"And it was time for them to go out and build houses of their own," said Sister.

"Exactly," said Mrs. Grizzle. "So the first little cub, who was inclined to be rather foolish, said, 'Since I love candy, I'm going to build my house of candy.'"

"Uh-oh!" said Brother.

"'Then I can have candy whenever I want!'" continued Mrs. Grizzle. "Then the second little cub, who was especially fond of cake, said, 'I shall build my house of cake. Then I can have cake whenever I want.'"

Cubs Brother and Sister were all ears.

"Now, that third little cub, who was a sensible sort, said, 'I like candy and cake as much as the next fellow, but I hear that the big bad pig has left his garbage dump and is on the prowl.'"

"Dum de dum dum," sang Sister.

"'And not only does the big bad pig have a terrific sweet tooth and terrible eating habits, he's known to have a taste for little cubs. Therefore, I'm going to build my house of logs—good solid logs.'"

Sister Bear began to look a little worried about what was going to happen, but Brother just grinned.

"So off they went to build their houses. Now, the big bad pig, who was indeed on the prowl—and what a disgusting, garbage-smelling fellow he was—came upon the house of the first little cub.

"'Yum!' he said. 'Little cub, little cub, let me in, or I'll snuffle and snort and burp your house in!'"

"I bet I know what the little cub is going to say," said Sister.

"Yeah," said Brother. "He's going to say 'Not by the hair of my chinny-chin-chin will I open the door and let you in.' Right?"

"'Not by the *fur* of my chinny-chin-chin,'" corrected Mrs. Grizzle. "But, hey, maybe you'd like to finish the story."

"No! Tell it! Tell it!" said Sister.

"Well, anyway, the big bad pig had already eaten his way through the candy wall, in the meantime, and was just about to clamp his mighty jaws on the first little cub.

"'Yipe!' cried the first little cub, and ran as fast as he could to the house of the second little cub, which you'll remember was made of cake."

"What kind of cake?" asked Sister.

"Oh, cupcakes, cinnamon buns, fudge cake—the whole bakery," said Mrs. Grizzle. "Well, after the big bad pig gobbled down all the first little cub's entire house of candy, he went to the house of the second little cub.

"'Open the door and let me in!' he roared. 'Or I'll snuffle and snort and burp your house in.'

"'Not by the fur of my chinny-chin-chin will I open the door and let you in!' said the second little cub.

"But that old pig had already eaten through the cake wall and was about to snap up the second *and* the first little cubs in his mighty jaws.

"'Yipe!' they cried. And they ran to the house of the third little cub, which you'll recall was made of logs.

"So the big bad pig gobbled down the whole bakery's worth of cake. Now, he still had one little cub to go. But he was beginning to feel a little sick."

"No wonder," said Sister. "He's eaten a whole house of candy and a whole house of cake!"

"Not to mention," said Brother, "all the garbage he usually ate."

"So when he got to the house of the third little cub, he was bent over with an awful bellyache. There was no shouting and demanding to be let in this time. He knocked politely on the door and said, 'Sir?'

"'Yes,' said the third little cub.

"'Please, sir,' said the big
bad pig. 'Do you happen to have a stomach
remedy in your medicine chest?'

"'Why, yes, I do,' said the third little cub. 'But I won't give it to you
unless you promise never ever to bother my brothers and me again.'

"'I promise! I promise!' groaned the big bad pig.

"So the third little cub pushed a big spoon of gooey pink stomach
medicine through the window.

"'Thank you! Thank you!' said the big bad pig as he licked the
spoon clean.

"And he kept his promise. He never ever bothered the three
little cubs again."

"That's a pretty good story, Mrs. Grizzle," said Brother.

"There's only one trouble with it," said Sister. "It made us hungry!"

"No problem," said Mrs. Grizzle. "I'll just scoot downstairs for some warm milk and cookies."

By the time she got back, the cubs were sound asleep.

IT WAS BEDTIME for Brother and Sister Bear again, and Mrs. Grizzle was babysitting. She settled down in her big, comfortable storytelling chair.

Goldibear and the Three People

"Long, long ago," she began, "in a land far, far away, there was a little cub named Goldibear."

"Goldibear?" said Sister. "That's a funny kind of name."

"She was called Goldibear," explained Mrs. Grizzle, "because her fur was such a bright golden brown."

"My fur looks sort of golden in the sunshine," said Sister, peeking at herself in the mirror near the bed.

Brother rolled his eyes.

"Now, Goldibear lived in a cottage in the forest," Mrs. Grizzle went on. "She was a curious little cub and liked to explore. But her mother was worried about her.

"'Goldibear,' she said one morning, 'it's all very well for you to go exploring in the forest. But you must never wander beyond the forest's borders.'

"'Why not?' asked Goldibear.

"'Because beyond the forest is a land where terrible creatures dwell!'

"'What kind of creatures?' asked Goldibear.

"'They are called People,' said her mother.

"'Why are they so terrible?' asked Goldibear.

"'I don't know,' said her mother. 'I've never seen them. But they are terrible, just the same!'

"With that, her mother left the cottage and went off to the honey store because they were getting low on wild berry honey.

"While her mother was out, Goldibear decided to go exploring. She skipped down the front steps of the cottage and out into the deep forest. She picked wildflowers, she chased butterflies, she played peekaboo with a woodpecker, and she ate some ripe blackberries.

"Before too long, she came to the edge of the forest. She peeked out and saw a pretty little house with a white picket fence nearby. It had roses around the door and a welcome mat on the front step. It looked so neat and tidy and inviting that her mother's warning about going beyond the borders of the forest never entered her head. Goldibear skipped right up the front path, hopped up the front steps, and knocked on the door. There was no answer.

"I'm sure the bears who live here won't mind if I take a look around their cute little house, thought Goldibear. Bold as you please, she opened the door and walked right in.

"But she did not realize that she was in the home of those terrible creatures, the Three People!"

"Oh no!" said Sister, shivering. She had heard weird stories about People when she was at summer camp and they used to sit around the campfire trying to scare one another all night.

"Hmmph!" said Brother skeptically, folding his arms. "I don't believe in People!" He had heard the stories too. But he wasn't scared . . . much.

"Now, Goldibear noticed three bowls of Cream of Wheat on the table," Mrs. Grizzle went on, "a great big one, a middle-sized one, and a wee baby one. She tasted the Cream of Wheat in the great big bowl. Ouch! It was too hot. She tasted the Cream of Wheat in

the middle-sized bowl. Ooh! It was too cold. Then she tasted the Cream of Wheat in the wee baby bowl. Yum! It was just right!"

"You know," interrupted Brother, "I've always wondered why the wee baby bowl wasn't colder than the middle-sized bowl. Wouldn't the smallest bowl cool off faster?"

Sister groaned.

"Now, Brother Bear," said Mrs. Grizzle, "don't go all nerdy on us."

"Me, nerdy?!" protested Brother, shocked.

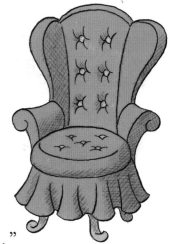

"Never mind," said Mrs. Grizzle. "Next, Goldibear tried sitting in the Three People's chairs. Umfph! The great big one was too hard. Squish! The middle-sized one was too soft. Ummm! The wee baby one was just right.

"But suddenly—you know what's coming next . . ."

"CRASH!" cried Brother and Sister. "It broke all to pieces!"

"Then Goldibear went upstairs to try the beds. First she tried Papa People's bed. Yuck! It was too scratchy. Then she tried Mama People's bed. Ugh! It was too lumpy. Then she tried wee little Baby People's bed. Ahh! It was just right. She climbed into bed, pulled the covers over her head, and went to sleep."

"How dumb can you get?" said Brother. "Breaking into the Three People's house, eating their food, breaking their furniture, and then taking a nap in their beds!"

"Yeah," said Sister. "I mean, it's just asking for trouble."

"Do you two want to hear this story or not?" asked Mrs. Grizzle.

"Tell it! Tell it!" said Brother and Sister.

"While Goldibear was sleeping, the Three People came home. The Three People looked at their bowls of Cream of Wheat.

"'Someone's been tasting my Cream of Wheat!' roared the Papa People in a great big voice.

"'Someone's been tasting *my* Cream of Wheat!' said the Mama People in a middle-sized voice.

"'Someone's been tasting *my* Cream of Wheat,' cried Baby People in a wee little voice . . .'"

"'And ate it all up!'" cried Brother and Sister in a wee little voice.

"The Three People looked at their chairs.

"'Someone's been sitting in my chair!' Papa People roared.

"'Someone's been sitting in *my* chair!' said Mama People.

"'Someone's been sitting in *my* chair,' wailed wee little Baby People . . .'"

"'And broke it all to pieces!'" wailed Brother and Sister.

"Then the Three People went upstairs to look around.

"Papa People roared again. 'Someone's been lying in my bed!'

"And Mama People said, 'Someone's been lying in *my* bed!'

"'Someone's been lying in *my* bed,' shouted Baby People . . ."

"'And *here she is!*'" shouted Brother and Sister Bear.

"All that roaring and shouting woke up Goldibear. She tossed the covers off and sat up in bed. Goldibear and the Three People stared at one another.

"'It's . . . A BEAR!' the Three People all shouted together.

"The Three People ran down the stairs, out the door, down the front path, and all the way to the police station, where they reported a bear invasion.

"Meanwhile, Goldibear stretched, climbed
out of bed, and made her way out of the house
and back to the forest, where she belonged."

"I think People are scary!" said Sister as Mrs.
Grizzle kissed them good night.

"Yeah," said Brother. "They're weird!"

"Don't worry," said Mrs. Grizzle. "None of them
live around here."

And she turned out the light.

SOMETHING THAT BROTHER AND SISTER really liked about Mrs. Grizzle was that she let them help in the kitchen when she babysat. One evening after she got Honey Bear to bed, Mrs. Grizzle baked gingerbread bears with Brother and Sister. Mrs. Grizzle made a big fancy one that they were going to save for tomorrow. Brother made a smaller one and decorated it with blue icing. Sister decorated hers with pink icing. They used currants for the eyes and raisins for buttons.

"I'm going to name mine Ginger Peachy," said Sister.

"I'm not going to name mine," said Brother.

"Why not?" asked Sister.

"Because that might make it harder to bite its head off!" said Brother.

"Hmm!" said Sister. "I didn't think of that."

"You can bite their heads off later," said Mrs. Grizzle. "It's time to clean up."

After the kitchen was clean and Brother and Sister had taken their baths, Brother and Sister took their gingerbread bears to bed with them.

"Since we have these tasty guests with us tonight," said Mrs. Grizzle, "maybe they'd like to hear the story of the gingerbread bear."

Brother and Sister pretended to talk for their gingerbread bears.

"Oh, yes, please, Mrs. Grizzle!" they said in high squeaky voices. "Tell it to us!"

"Not so loud!" said Mrs. Grizzle. "You'll wake up Honey Bear."

"Please tell it!" they repeated in quieter voices.

"Very well," said Mrs. Grizzle.

The Gingerbread Bear

"Once in a little old house in the woods, there lived a little old grandma bear and a little old grandpa bear."

"Just like our Grizzly Gramps and Gran," said Sister Bear.

"One day, the grandma bear baked a gingerbread bear with currants for eyes and raisins for buttons."

"Just like us!" said Brother's and Sister's gingerbread bears in their high squeaky voices.

"But before the grandma bear could take the gingerbread bear out of the pan, he jumped up, bounced out the door, and ran down the path.

"'Stop! Stop!' cried the little old grandma bear and the little old grandpa bear, running after him into the woods.

"But the gingerbread bear laughed and said—"

"We know this part!" Brother and Sister chimed in:

"'Run, run, as fast as you dare!
You can't catch me,
I'm the gingerbread bear!'"

"He ran past a long-eared rabbit and a furry raccoon.

"'Stop! Stop!' they called.

"But the gingerbread bear laughed again and said:

"'Run, run, as fast as you dare!
You can't catch me,
I'm the gingerbread bear!
I ran away from the grandma bear
And the grandpa bear,
And I can run away from you!
So, there!'

"Next he ran past a woodcutter, who dropped his ax and joined the chase. The gingerbread bear laughed at him and said:

"'Run, run, as fast as you dare!
You can't catch me,
I'm the gingerbread bear!
I ran away from the grandma bear
and the grandpa bear,
the long-eared rabbit
and the furry raccoon,
And I can run away from you!
So, there!'

"And he did, until he came to a stream that
was too wide to cross without getting soggy.
"'Jump onto my tail!' offered a sly fox,
wading into the stream.

"'Since your tail is so far from your mouth, I shall!' said the gingerbread bear. And he jumped on the tip of the fox's nice dry tail for the ride across."

"Bad move! Bad move!" squeaked the cubs' gingerbread bears.

"But the stream was deep, and the fox's tail soon got wet. 'Jump on my back!' said the sly fox.

"Next thing you know, his back was in the water too. The gingerbread bear jumped to the fox's head, and then to his nose. Snip, snap—the fox ate him up!"

Mrs. Grizzle suddenly noticed that Brother's and Sister's gingerbread bears were strangely silent.

"What happened to your gingerbread bears?" she asked.

Brother and Sister grinned sheepishly and held out their hands. There was nothing left but some gingerbread crumbs.

"When you got to the part about the fox going 'snip, snap,' we couldn't resist," said Brother.

"Well, after all," said Mrs. Grizzle, "that's what gingerbread bears are for."

Sister Bear just licked her lips.

"HOW ABOUT 'The Three Billy Goats Gruff'?" asked Mrs. Grizzle one evening at story time.

"Nah!" said Brother. "I get tired of all that *'Trip, trap! Trip, trap! Over the bridge'* stuff."

"And I don't like that awful old troll," said Sister. "He's scary!"

"Have you ever heard the story of 'The Three Billy Goats Gruff Meet the Bogg Brothers'?" asked Mrs. Grizzle.

"No," said Brother and Sister. It sounded interesting. "Tell it!" they said.

"If you insist," said Mrs. Grizzle.

The Three Billy Goats Gruff
Meet the Bogg Brothers

"There once were three goat brothers named the Three Billy Goats Gruff. They lived in a pasture on one side of a valley. On the other side of the valley, there was a hill where grew the richest and greenest grass that any goat had ever seen. The Three Billy Goats Gruff longed to go eat that rich green grass. But to get across the valley, they would have to cross a bridge over a stream. And under that bridge lived the Bogg Brothers."

"Who were they?" wondered Sister.

"The Bogg Brothers were three of the meanest, scruffiest, orneriest bears in all of Bear Country. They planted themselves under that bridge and wouldn't let anybody get across without their say-so. And they had a hankering for a taste of some nice, hot goat stew!"

"Oh, dear!" said Sister. The Bogg Brothers sounded almost as scary as that awful old troll.

"Well, one day the smallest of the Three Billy Goats Gruff couldn't resist all that luscious green grass on the other side of the valley. He set off to cross the bridge over the stream.

"*Trip, trap! Trip, trap!* went his small hooves on the bridge.

"The Bogg Brothers looked up when they heard the sound.

"'WHO'S THAT CROSSING OUR BRIDGE?' yelled Clem, the youngest Bogg Brother.

"'It's me, the smallest Billy Goat Gruff,' said the young goat.

"'Git out the smallest pot, boys!' said Clem. 'Peel up some potaters and slice up some turnips. It's goat stew tonight, for sure!' And he started to climb up to the bridge to grab the goat.

"But the smallest Billy Goat Gruff said, 'My older brother is much bigger than I am. If you wait for him to cross the bridge, I'm sure he'd make a better meal.'"

"Nice brother!" said Sister.

"I'd do the same for you," said Brother.

"Thanks," said Sister.

"Clem thought this sounded like a good idea, so he let the smallest Billy Goat Gruff cross the bridge. Soon he was eating the rich grass on the other side of the valley.

"Before too long, the middle-sized Billy Goat Gruff decided that he wanted to try the grass on the other side of the valley as well. He set out to cross the bridge.

"*Trip, trap! Trip, trap!* went his middle-sized hooves on the bridge.

"'WHO'S THAT CROSSING OUR BRIDGE?' yelled Lem, the middle Bogg Brother.

"'It's me,' said the Billy Goat, 'the middle-sized Billy Goat Gruff.'

"'Git out the middle-sized pot, boys!' said Lem. 'Mince up some parsley and dice some parsnips. It's goat stew tonight, for sure!' And he started to climb up to the bridge to grab the goat.

"But the middle-sized Billy Goat Gruff said, 'My older brother is much bigger than I am. If you wait for him to cross the bridge, I'm sure he'd make a better meal.'

"This sounded just fine to Lem. So he let the middle-sized Billy Goat Gruff cross the bridge. Soon he was eating the delicious grass on the hillside too."

"What's a parsnip?" asked Sister.

"It's a root vegetable," said Mrs. Grizzle.

"What's it look like?" asked Brother.

"Sort of like a big white carrot," said Mrs. Grizzle.

"EW!" said Brother and Sister.

"Anyway, before too long the biggest Billy Goat Gruff decided to try the grass on the other side of the valley. He, too, set off to cross the bridge.

"TRIP, TRAP! TRIP, TRAP! went his big hooves on the bridge.

"'WHO'S THAT CROSSING OUR BRIDGE?' yelled Shem, the oldest Bogg Brother.

"'It's me,' said the Billy Goat, 'the biggest Billy Goat Gruff.'

"'Git out the biggest pot, boys!' said Shem. 'Go find the bay leaves and the mint jelly. It's goat stew tonight, for sure!' And he climbed right up onto the bridge with the biggest Billy Goat Gruff. Clem and Lem grabbed their guns and climbed up with him."

"I love mint jelly," said Sister.

"Me too!" said Brother, licking his lips. "With lamb—I guess it would taste good with goat too."

"I wouldn't want to eat a goat!" said Sister, making a face.

Brother thought about it.

"Yuck!" he agreed.

"The Bogg Brothers didn't think so," said Mrs. Grizzle. "They climbed up on that bridge, looked at the biggest Billy Goat Gruff, and smacked their lips.

"'Ain't you the big juicy one!' said Shem.

"'Sure enough!' said Lem. 'You'll make more'n a mouthful or two!'

"'An' how!' said Clem. 'I sure do admire a nice bowl of goat stew for supper!'

"But the biggest Billy Goat Gruff was not the least bit frightened. He just lowered his long, sharp, curved horns, pawed the bridge with his front hooves, and charged! He ran right into the Bogg Brothers and butted them off the bridge into the stream below. They fell into the water with an enormous splash.

"And the biggest Billy Goat Gruff crossed the bridge to join his brothers eating the rich green grass on the other side of the valley."

"What do parsnips taste like?" asked Sister as Mrs. Grizzle tucked the cubs in.

"Not much," said Mrs. Grizzle, kissing them good night.

"Are they good with mint jelly?" asked Brother, closing his eyes.

"Everything's good with mint jelly," said Mrs. Grizzle. "Good night!"

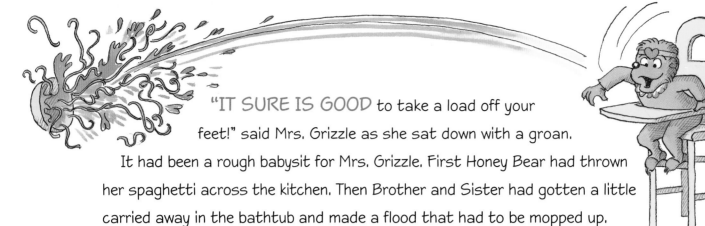

"IT SURE IS GOOD to take a load off your feet!" said Mrs. Grizzle as she sat down with a groan.

It had been a rough babysit for Mrs. Grizzle. First Honey Bear had thrown her spaghetti across the kitchen. Then Brother and Sister had gotten a little carried away in the bathtub and made a flood that had to be mopped up.

She sighed. "I'm bushed!"

"Does that mean you're too tired to tell us a bedtime story?" asked Sister Bear.

"Not at all." Mrs. Grizzle smiled. "But it does mean that I'm going to make it a quick one—okay?"

"Okay," said Brother.

"But make it a good one," added Sister.

"A good-and-quick one!" said Mrs. Grizzle.

The Little Red Hen

"One day when the little red hen was scratching in the barnyard, she found some grains of wheat.

"'Who will help me plant this wheat?' she asked.

"'I will!' said the duck.

"'I will!' said the cat.

"'I will!' said the pig.

"'Then I'll go and relax while you three plant it,' said the little red hen. And she did."

"That's not how the story goes!" said Sister.

"No!" said Brother. "They're all supposed to say, 'Not I!'"

"And the little red hen is supposed to say, 'Then I will do it myself!'"

"This is the good-and-quick version," said Mrs. Grizzle.

"Oh," said Sister and Brother doubtfully.

"The wheat sprouted and grew into tall stalks.

"'Who will help me cut the wheat?' asked the little red hen.

"'I will!' said the duck.

"'I will!' said the cat.

"'I will!' said the pig.

"'Good,' said the little red hen. 'I think I'll go watch *American Turkey Idol* on TV.' And she did."

"Mrs. Grizzle," said Sister, "are you sure this is how the good-and-quick version goes?"

"Trust me," said Mrs. Grizzle.

"On the wheat stalks there were ripe heads of grain.

"'Who will help me thresh the wheat?' asked the little red hen.

"'I will!' said the duck.

"'I will!' said the cat.

"'I will!' said the pig.

"'Okay,' said the little red hen. 'I'm gonna go take a little nap.' And she
    did."

"This can't be how it goes," muttered Brother to Sister.

"What's that?" asked Mrs. Grizzle.

"Nothing," said Brother.

"Soon the little red hen had a sack of grain.

"'Who will help me take the wheat to the mill?' she asked.

"'I will!' said the duck.

"'I will!' said the cat.

"'I will!' said the pig.

"'Terrific!' said the little red hen. 'I'll just have time to get down to the big sale at the Poultry Mall before you're done.' And she did."

Brother and Sister just looked at each other and shrugged.

"The mill ground the wheat into flour.

"'Who will help me bake the bread?' asked the little red hen.

"'I will!' said the duck.

"'I will!' said the cat.

"'I will!' said the pig.

"'Swell,' said the little red hen. 'I'm going to my Avian Aerobics class for a while.' And she did."

Brother and Sister didn't even bother to say anything.

"When the little red hen got back from her Avian Aerobics class, the duck, the cat, and the pig had baked a beautiful loaf of bread.

"'Now, who will help me eat the bread?' asked the little red hen.

"'Not I,' said the duck.

"'Not I,' said the cat.

"'Not I,' said the pig.

"'Why not?' asked the little red hen.

"'Because we're allergic to wheat, that's why not!' they all said."

"Mrs. Grizzle," said Brother.

"Yes?" she said.

"That was the dumbest story I've ever heard," he said.

"Oh?" said Mrs. Grizzle. "What do you think, Sister?"

Sister held her nose and turned her thumb down.

"Well," said Mrs. Grizzle, tucking them in and turning out the light, "I'm too tired to argue about it. Good night!"

"Phooey!" muttered Brother, rolling over to go to sleep.

"Yeah," whispered Sister. "Double phooey!"

"YOU KNOW WHAT my own favorite bedtime story is?" asked Mrs. Grizzle one evening when she was babysitting.

"No, what?" asked Brother and Sister, snuggling down in their beds.

"'Little Red Grizzly Hood,'" said Mrs. Grizzle.

"Is that different from 'Little Red Riding Hood'?" asked Sister.

"Do you want to find out?" asked Mrs. Grizzle.

Brother and Sister nodded. "Okay."

Little Red Grizzly Hood

"Once there was a little cub whose grandmother loved her very much. She made her grandcub a beautiful red cape with a hood. The little cub loved the cape and wore it everywhere. So she became known as Little Red Grizzly Hood."

"Weird name!" said Brother.

"I had a Snow White costume for Halloween that had a cape," said Sister. "But it didn't have a hood."

"I was the Headless Horsebear that year," said Brother. "That was a cool costume! The trick-or-treat bag was a jack-o'-lantern!"

"Shall I continue?" asked Mrs. Grizzle.

"Please!" said Brother and Sister politely.

"One day Little Red Grizzly Hood's grandmother fell ill. The little cub's mother packed a basket of goodies and gave it to Little Red Grizzly Hood to take to her grandmother. The cub set off cheerfully through the forest."

"What kind of goodies?" asked Sister.

"Oh, chicken salad, cheese and crackers, some sliced-up pineapple, a thermos of tea, a couple of cookies," said Mrs. Grizzle.

"No cake?" asked Brother.

"Well, after all," said Mrs. Grizzle, "the old lady was sick."

"Oh, yeah," said Brother.

"Now, Little Red Grizzly Hood had not gone far into the forest when she met a wolf.

"'Good afternoon, my dear!' said the wolf. 'Where are you off to this fine day, may I ask?'

"'I'm going to take this basket of goodies to my grandmother, who is sick,' said Little Red Grizzly Hood.

"The wolf smiled. 'How thoughtful. Have a pleasant journey!'

"And the little cub continued on her way. But the wolf sneaked past her and ran all the way to the grandmother's cottage ahead of her. The grandmother spied the wolf coming and hid in a cupboard. The wolf came inside but could not find her. So he put on the grandmother's nightcap and climbed into her bed to wait for Little Red Grizzly Hood.

"Soon the cub arrived at the cottage. She saw that the door was open, so she let herself in. She came right up to the wolf in her grandmother's bed.

"'Hello, Grandmother,' she said.

"'Hello, my dear!' said the wolf in a high, creaky voice.

"Little Red Grizzly Hood thought that her grandmother looked terrible—she must really be sick!

"'Why, Grandmother,' she said, 'what big ears you have!'"

Brother and Sister broke in:

"'The better to hear you with, my dear!'" they said in high, creaky voices.

"'Why, Grandmother,' said the cub, 'what big eyes you have!'"

" 'The better to see you with, my dear!' " creaked Brother and Sister.

" 'And Grandmother,' said the cub, 'what big teeth you have!' "

" 'The better to eat you with!' " roared Brother and Sister.

"The wolf leaped from the bed and tried to catch Little Red Grizzly
Hood. But the cub ran outside shouting for help. A woodcutter
happened to be passing and heard her cries. He ran into the cottage and,
waving his ax, chased the wolf back into the forest.

"Little Red Grizzly Hood heard a knocking from the cupboard. She opened it and let her grandmother out of her hiding place. Then she and her grandmother and the woodcutter sat down to eat the basket of goodies. They made her grandmother feel much better."

"I like that story," said Sister as she hugged her snoozer doll.

"Me too," said Brother, taking his stuffed dog, Poochie, out from under his pillow, where he hid him. "Why is it your favorite, Mrs. Grizzle?"

"Because," she said, kissing them good night and turning out the light, "my babysitter used to tell it to me when I was a girl."

"Oh," said Brother thoughtfully.

Sister was already asleep.